You Can't Teach an Old Dad New Jokes:

Mr. Harold's Illustrated Jokes and More, More, More!!!

Written by:

"Mr." Harold Newcomb

Editing & Development: Brent K. Newcomb

Art by: Scorpy Designs & Brent K. Newcomb

Cover by: Eli Ilnaz

You Can't Teach an Old Dad New Jokes:

Mr. Harold's Illustrated Jokes and More, More, More!!!

ISBN 978-1-959402-00-8

You Can't Teach an Old Dad New Jokes:

Mr. Harold's Illustrated Jokes and More, More, More!!!

Who is Mr. Harold?

(Intro by the Author)

Hey, guys! Thanks for buying my book, *You Can't Teach an Old Dad New Jokes: Mr. Harold's Illustrated Jokes and More, More, More!* I'm sure you're going to find some gems (and possibly some duds here). But that's the fun. Life is basically a cycle of hearing a large number of jokes and whittling it down to the ones we like the most, and then repeating those to everyone we know. And that's what you have here.

But how did I get started in the joke business? Well, it started strangely enough on a sharecropper farm in the late 1930s. I was a small child, the fifth of seven children. This meant that I got many of my first jokes as a fourth hand-me-down. (I just feel sorry for my younger siblings.)

Of course, at that time we didn't have electricity, so my older brother made a TV out of an old orange crate. When I raised an eyebrow at this, he said it didn't work because we were too far away to get any good stations. At the time I didn't see any humor in that as I stared at the crate. But looking back I should have just asked him to move the crate for better reception.

Other pranks I endured at that tender age included the "stick-and-wet-britches" gag, the "I-can-see-the-wind" gag, and the "you-can-fly-if-you-jump-off-this-roof-and-flap-hard-enough" gag. With each loud guffaw of my six brothers and sisters, I was transforming, evolving, becoming Mr. Harold, the guy who would make his own pranks and jokes.

Before long I found myself in the Army under the GI Bill which would help me pay for college. I watched all the war movies and TV shows I could find to help me prepare. As luck would have it, I found myself keenly drawn to the antics of 1958's "No Time for Sergeants," starring Andy Griffith and Don Knotts. There was no avoiding the spiral into total zaniness after that.

I tested my wit at Foot Hood, Texas while standing in formation with hundreds of other men. My drill sergeant asked whether anyone in the camp had "prior" experience. Being from "Pryor," Oklahoma, I didn't miss a beat when I raised my hand. I was ordered to march the men to the chow hall for lunch. Of course, I didn't know how to march men, so I just said, "Come on boys, let's go eat!" After the laughter died down and I had explained what I meant by "Pryor" experience, the sergeant knew he had a live one. This is when the men first started calling me Mr. Harold, a moniker I wear proudly to this day.

I do hope you enjoy this illustrated sampling of my life's collection of humor. I've told these same jokes for over fifty years and have honed them to perfection. Before I can even get three words out of my mouth, my two boys (who are now quite grown up) tell the punchline and don't even groan anymore. And that's when you know you've made a mark in life.

But remember, I may be funny, but my jokes are not to be laughed at.

Yours truly,

Mr. Harold!!!

1.

Betty Joe bought a baby buggy one day. However, poor Betty didn't have a baby, so she put her little doggy, Fido, in the baby buggy and pushed it around. A few months passed and she had a baby and didn't know what to do with it. She kept Fido in the buggy but put the baby on a leash. This didn't work out as well as she'd hoped, so she took the doggy out of the buggy and put her baby in. Instead of a baby buggy, she now has a Buggy Baby.

***

Betty Joe was pushing her baby buggy through the park. An old lady came up to her and said, "My, oh, my, what a cute baby! What sign was he conceived under?"

Betty Joe blushed and replied, "Keep off the grass!"

2.

Mr. Harold loves to recite the following tale:

The Man in the moon,

As he sailed through the skies,

Was a very remarkable skipper.

But he made a mistake,

When he tried to take,

A drink of milk from the Dipper.

He took a big dip,

Cuz' he wanted a sip,

Of the Milky Way to fill it.

But the Big Bear growled,

And the Little Bear howled,

And scared him so much that he spilt' it.

3.

One day, Mr. Harold was sitting in prison serving several years for telling bad jokes about the Judge's wife. He was lonely and could only think about leaving. About that time a small ant crawled across the floor. Mr. Harold's life changed at that moment. He took the little ant, named him Petey, and started to train him. He taught him back flips, how to jump through his fingers, how to juggle breadcrumbs, and even how to sing and dance. He was so proud. He knew that he would take the little ant on the road and make a lot of money with him once he was released.

And the day came when Mr. Harold was free. He took the little ant and headed to a bar to get a drink before embarking on his whirlwind novelty act tour. He sat on a stool and put Petey on the table and promptly ordered a whiskey for himself and for the little. The bartender turned around with the two shot glasses, placed them on the counter, and promptly squished the ant that he saw crawling on the table. "Here ya' go, Mack," he said. "And where's your friend Petey?"

4.

Being distraught and lonely, Mr. Harold walked into a pet shop looking for a new companion. But all that the pet store had that day was a centipede named Charley. Mr. Harold didn't mind and took Charley home.

The two got along splendidly until Sunday morning when it was time for church. Mr. Harold asked the centipede, "Hey, Charley, you wanna' to go to Sunday School with me?"

The centipede said only, "Just a sec."

Mr. Harold called out a little louder, "Mr. Centipede, it's Sunday. Do you want to go to Sunday School with me?"

The centipede said again, "Just a sec."

So, Mr. Harold, a bit red in the face, hollered even louder, "Hey, Charley! You comin' with me to Sunday School or not?"

Charley called back, frustrated, "I heard you the first time. I said just a sec. I'm putting on my darn shoes!"

5.

Sensing his son was a little naïve, Mr. Harold asked Lil' Bobby, "If a Papa Bull could eat three bales of hay in one week, and a Baby Bull could eat one bale of hay in one week, how much hay could a Mama Bull eat in one week?"

Lil' Bobby answered, "Umm...two?"

Mr. Harold laughed, "That's ridiculous. There's no such thing as a mama bull, only a mama cow!"

A few minutes went by and Mr. Harold then asked his son, "What do you call a bull that's lying down?"

Lil' Bobby couldn't answer.

"Ground beef!"

His son was perplexed so Mr. Harold wanted to try a third question, "Son, how does a bull introduce his wife?"

"Dunno..."

"Meat Patty!"

Lil' Bobby still did not understand.

Mr. Harold then said, "I think it's *pasture* bedtime."

6.

One fine Sunday, Betty Joe invited the preacher to Sunday lunch after church. But on the way home, she admonished her children to behave. "Silly Suzie, I know you have a habit of scratching yourself all over and without a break, but you'd better not do that in front of the preacher!"

Silly Suzie struggled not to scratch and said, "Yes, mama."

"And Lil' Bobby, you'd better not wipe your nose with your sleeves, or you'll get a proper whoopin'!"

Lil' Bobby, whose nose was running at that moment, simply said, "Yes, mama."

The lunch was terrific, and the preacher was satisfied, but the two children struggled mightily not to misbehave. It was too much for Silly Suzie. She itched as she'd never itched before. So as not to disappoint her mother, she said, "Preacher? Mama's gonna' make me a new spotted dress."

The Preacher said, "Is that so?"

Silly Suzie began to scratch all over, "And there's gonna' be a spot here…and one here…and one here…"

Lil' Bobby's nose was running so much by that point that he, too, had to do something. Wiping his nose with his sleeve as he pointed,

Lil' Bobby said, "Preacher? See that picture over there?" Then wiping his nose with his other sleeve as he pointed, "Mama's gonna' move it over there!"

7.

One day Mr. Harold was arrested in a foreign country for telling bad jokes. His sentence? Firing squad. On the day of the execution, two other guys were scheduled to be shot as well. The first guy was placed against the pole. The soldiers aimed their rifles and the commander said, "Ready!... Aim!..."

But before he could finish, the man yelled, "Earthquake!" The soldiers were so scared, that they dropped their weapons and ran, allowing him to escape.

When they realized they had been fooled, they placed the second man against the pole and raised their weapons. Again, "Ready!... Aim!...."

But before the command could be given, the second man yelled, "Avalanche!" The soldiers were so frightened that they scattered, allowing the second man to escape like the first.

Not to be outdone, when it was Mr. Harold's turn, he was ready. The soldiers raised their weapons. The commander said, "Ready!... Aim!..."

Mr. Harold then yelled, "Fire!"

8.

Mr. Harold loves to tell the following tale:

A rich girl uses face cream,

A poor girl uses lard,

My gal uses axle grease and rubs it extra hard.

A rich girl drives a limousine,

A poor girl drives a Ford,

My gal rides an old gray mare and beats her with a board.

***

When everyone has quit laughing, Mr. Harold then usually asks, "What has six legs, four eyes, two heads, and a tail?"

"A woman sitting on a donkey."

9.

When asked about his thoughts on unattractive women, Mr. Harold always says:

"Some people say 'Beauty' is only skin deep. That may be true. But 'Ugly' goes clean to the bone."

***

One day Betty Joe asked her husband, "Am I pretty or ugly?"

Mr. Harold replied, "You're both."

"What do you mean?" she asked.

"You're pretty ugly."

***

Once upon a time, Mr. Harold met a woman whose teeth were like stars…They came out at night. She had pretty blue eyes…. One blew this way, and one blew that way. She had long beautiful hair… from her armpits. Her portraits were so ugly that they hung themselves.

10.

Mr. Harold wanted to test Lil' Bobby again. He asked, "Son, what gets larger the more you take away from it?"

Lil' Bobby thought and thought but could come up with no answer.

Mr. Harold crossed his arms and proudly said, "A hole."

***

His son was perplexed, so he followed up with this zinger: "Son, what gives milk, has a horn, but is not a cow?"

Lil' Bobby couldn't answer.

"A milk truck, my boy."

***

Finally, Mr. Harold teased his son further, "Boy, what is orange and sounds like a parrot?"

"I dunno."

"A carrot."

11.

One fine day, Mr. Harold entered a diner and smiled at the waitress behind the counter. He asked, "May I please have a cup of black coffee without cream?"

The clever waitress knew of Mr. Harold's penchant for jokes and replied, "We are all out of cream, unfortunately. Would you take it without milk?"

***

Not to be outdone, Mr. Harold pointed to a sign that said, "Breakfast served at any time."

He said, "I'd like French toast during the Dark Ages.

***

When the waitress didn't laugh, he asked, "How much is a soft drink?"

She replied, "One dollar, but refills are free."

Mr. Harold said, "Well, then, I'll just have a refill."

12.

When feeling especially feisty, Mr. Harold likes to recite the following:

A raccoon's tail has rings all around,

An opossum's tail is bare,

But a rabbit has no tail at all,

Just an itty-bitty bundle of hair.

***

Mr. Harold asked his son, "Why did the raccoon cross the road?"

Lil' Bobby answered, "To prove to the opossum that it could be done!"

***

"And why did the raccoon go 'Moo'?"

Lil' Bobby answered quicker than ever, "Cuz' it was learning a new language!"

13.

Life can be very hectic, and Mr. Harold knows this better than anyone. But when things get too crazy, he remembers:

"Even the snail and the turtle made it to the ark on time."

"When you get caught napping at work, just raise your head and say, 'In Jesus' name, amen.'"

"If you get a loan at a bank, you pay for it for thirty years. But if you rob a bank, you're out in ten."

"If you sleep until lunchtime, you can save money on breakfast."

"Trade in your house for a motorhome. Kids won't move back home if they can't find it."

14.

One day Mr. Harold and his son were coming out of Sunday School. But he wasn't sure whether Lil' Bobby and Silly Suzie had paid attention.

He asked, "What did you learn about today?"

Silly Suzie answered, "We learned that in the Bible, God told Noah to build an ark."

Mr. Harold replied, "Very good. And what did you learn, Lil' Bobby?

Lil' Bobby thought awhile and answered, "Well, all the animals entered the ark in pairs."

Mr. Harold replied, "Almost. You forgot about the worms."

Both children asked, "What about the worms?"

Mr. Harold beamed and said, "They came in apples, not pears."

15.

One day Mr. Harold saw his son laughing and laughing under a tree. He asked Lil' Bobby, "What's so funny? I'd like in on the joke."

Lil' Bobby answered with a question, "What is red in the middle and green on top, and makes your tongue go flippity-flop?" Before his dad could answer, Lil' Bobby quickly said, "A watermelon!"

Mr. Harold shrugged his shoulders, "Let me ask you, what vegetables can make you cry?"

Lil' Bobby thought and thought, "An onion?"

Mr. Harold, "A watermelon … especially if I throw it at you!"

Lil' Bobby didn't ask any more dumb questions that day.

16.

Silly Suzie asked her father, Mr. Harold, "Have you heard about the Blind Carpenter who was healed? He picked up his hammer and *saw*."

Not to be outdone, Mr. Harold asked her, "Did you hear about the engineer, the carpenter, and the statistician who went hunting? The engineer shot at a deer but missed and said, 'Darn, two yards to the left.' The carpenter shot, missed, and said, 'Darn, two yards to the right.' The statistician jumped up and exclaimed, 'Wow! Looks like we got him!'"

***

Mr. Harold was complaining to his preacher about the carpenter. "Yes, I told him I didn't want carpeted steps!"

The preacher asked, "What did he say?"

Mr. Harold smiled and said, "He gave me a blank stair!"

17.

One day, Mr. Harold went to see an eye specialist for an eye exam. The Doctor asked him, "Have your eyes been checked lately?"

Mr. Harold, nonplussed, answered, "No, they've always been this color."

***

After informing him that he will need an operation, Mr. Harold replied, "Doctor, after the procedure, will I be able to play the piano?"

The doctor said, "I don't see why not."

Mr. Harold smiled, "That's terrific! I never could play before!"

18.

Not long afterward, Mr. Harold went to a service station and bought a quart of oil. The young gas station attendant asked him, "Are you going to put this in yourself?"

Mr. Harold answered with a sly smile, "Nope, I'm going to put it in my car."

***

While he was still at the station Mr. Harold asked, "Can you tell me why my car is humming"

The mechanic replied with a smile, "Probably cuz' it doesn't know the words."

***

Before he left, the mechanic asked Mr. Harold if he needed anything else.

"I want a gas cap for my car."

"I think that's a fair trade," replied the mechanic.

19.

Mr. Harold asked his witless son, "Boy, how many three-cent stamps are there in a dozen?"

Lil' Bobby couldn't answer.

Mr. Harold then asked, "What is heavier, a ton of feathers or a ton of bricks?"

Lil' Bobby couldn't answer.

Finally, Mr. Harold asked his son to repeat the following words: silk, jilk, dilk, filk." After Lil' Bobby did so, he asked, "And what do cows drink?"

Lil' Bobby answered proudly, "Milk!"

Mr. Harold smiled, "Um…they drink water, son…"

20.

When you catch Mr. Harold waxing nostalgic, he'll repeat this ditty:

Thirty days hath September,

April, June, and No Wonder,

All the rest eat peanut butter,

Except for Gramma. She drives a Buick.

***

When no one laughs, he'll try this one out:

Birdie, birdie in the sky,

Dropped some white stuff in my eye,

I'm a big boy. I won't cry.

I'm just glad that cows can't fly.

21.

Lil' Bobby's teacher asked him to write a poem that rhymed. It took him more than a week, but he wrote the following:

Roses are red,

Violets are blue,

Gramma's undies are fine,

I saw 'em hangin' on the line.

Roses are red,

Violets are blue,

When I listen to rock music,

My neighbors do, too.

Roses are red,

Violets are blue,

Sunflowers are yellow,

Hey, teach, I'm not a gardener or a poet, obviously!

22.

And when things get a little too serious, Mr. Harold loves to tell the following tale:

One midnight on the ocean blue, not a streetcar was in sight,

The ocean was so dusty cuz' it'd rained all day and all that night,

Two young boys got up to fight. Back-to-back they stood,

They drew their swords quite promptly and shot each other good.

A deaf policeman heard the noise and came to see the sight,

He arrested the two dead boys, and the case was closed that night.

If you don't believe this winding tale, if you don't think it's true,

Ask the blind man over there, he saw it all play through.

23.

Once again Mr. Harold thought his son, Lil' Bobby was soft in the head. "Come here, son," he beckoned.

"Yes, papa!"

"Answer me this:

Three Old Kings came riding by,

They saw three pair hanging high,

Each King took a pear,

But left three pear hanging there."

***

Mr. Harold likes to stump his son with the following:

"Which of King Arthur's knights invented the round table?"

When Lil' Bobby didn't answer, Mr. Harold said, "Sir Cumference, of course!"

24.

Once on a warm summer's eve, Mr. Harold was playing catcher in a local softball league when a fabulous horse came up to bat. Mr. Harold knew the horse was fast, could catch like a pro, and could cover the entire outfield. It was the 9th inning, and the score was tied with two out. The horse swung his bat a few times awaiting the pitch. Pow! The horse whacked a home run well over the fence. But the horse refused to run the bases. Mr. Harold had no choice but to call him out.

Eventually, the horse's team lost the game in extra innings. The horse's manager asked the horse why he had refused to run the bases and win the game. The horse replied, "Now wouldn't that look stupid, a horse running the bases?"

25.

Silly Suzie was sitting in the park and scratching her head. A kindly gentleman approached her and asked, "What's wrong, darling?"

"Well, I was standing here and thinking about all those people who run back and forth."

The gentleman asked, "And what's wrong with that?"

Silly Suzie replied, "Everyone knows you have to run forth first before you can come back."

***

Silly Suzie was in a pizza parlor and ordered a pizza.

The waitress asked, "Would you like that cut into six pieces or eight?"

Silly Suzie replied, "Six pieces. I could never eat eight!"

26.

Mr. Harold asked his less-than-bright son, "When a person has a growth removed from his throat, what's it called?"

Lil' Bobby answered, "A tonsillectomy, dad."

He followed this up with, "And when a person has a growth removed from his body, what's that called?"

Lil' Bobby beamed, "An appendectomy!"

"And what if a person has a growth removed from his head?"

Lil' Bobby couldn't answer.

Mr. Harold smiled, "A haircut, son…a haircut."

27.

Mr. Harold was building a house and his budget was limited. He went to a local home improvement store and ordered exactly enough materials so that not a single thing would be wasted; every nail and screw and bolt should be used.

After taking all the items purchased, he began work on the house. It took several days, but finally, it was finished. However, to Mr. Harold's surprise, there was a single brick left over. Mr. Harold was distraught. What was he going to do? He thought and thought about it, but alas, he had no answer.

A passerby saw Mr. Harold, dejected, sitting near his new home, brick in hand. "What's the trouble, sir?" the man asked.

Mr. Harold responded, "Well, I have this brick here left over and I don't know what to do with it."

The man calmly said, "Well, do what we used to do in my day, just throw it up in the air and forget about it."

And so Mr. Harold did just that, never to be bothered about the brick again.

28.

One fall day, Mr. Harold was sitting in an airplane taking a trip across the country. Next to him was a very annoying lady with a tiny dog, no bigger than her purse, yapping away incessantly. The yapping went on and on, much to Mr. Harold's distress.

When he couldn't take it anymore, Mr. Harold pulled out a thick cigar, lit it, and started puffing away, blowing the smoke towards the lady with the barking dog. The lady asked him to put away the foul cigar. Mr. Harold refused until the dog quit its yapping.

Neither person budged. Unfortunately, Mr. Harold could not take it anymore and he picked up the dog and tossed him out of the plane window. The woman was incensed and yanked the cigar from Mr. Harold's mouth and threw it out the window.

Eventually, the plane landed with the two angry passengers. When they got out of the plane they looked up and saw the little dog running up to them with something in its mouth. Can you guess what it was???

A brick.

29.

One bright Sunday Betty Joe and Mr. Harold invited the family preacher for Sunday dinner. Of course, they were worried that their two children, Lil' Bobby and Silly Suzie would act out. Betty Joe admonished them. "Children," she said, "I want you to be on your best behavior. I want you to scrub up squeaky clean, I want you to say please and thank you, and most of all, I don't want you to use your hands to grab any food on the table. Politeness is next to Godliness," she told them.

"Yes, mama," they replied.

"And that goes for you, too, Mr. Harold!"

"Yes, dear."

Around the dinner table sat the family along with the preacher in his black and white Sunday suit. The table looked beautiful, with plates of food, and in the center, a stack of exactly 6 steaks, one for each person at the table plus one extra (just in case).

Everyone gorged himself on all the food and each had his own steak. But there was this one steak left over. Everyone wanted it, but no one dared to be impolite as Betty Joe was watching them all like a hawk. Just when the tension couldn't get any higher, the lights went out and it became pitch dark. There was a shriek.

When the lights came on, the poor preacher's hand was hovering above the last steak with four forks stuck in it.

30.

One day at the vet, several animals sat and waited for their appointments, each moaning and in pain. The poor giraffe had a sore throat. The ill-tempered elephant had a runny nose. A cow had hay fever. A frog had warts. An alligator had dry skin. A camel had two pains in his back. The snake needed a calculator as he wasn't a good adder. The panda was cold because he had bear feet. But worst of all, a cow was crying over some spilled milk.

***

Mr. Harold asked the vet, "What do you get when you cross and elephant with a rhino?"

The vet shrugged his shoulders and said, "Elephino!"

31.

One day, Mr. Harold was building a house and he was hard at work. He had a hammer in one hand and a box of nails beside him as he worked. Every so often, he would scrutinize a nail, furl his lips, then drop one of the nails into another box he had nearby. He would then proceed to the next nail. If it met his scrutiny, he used it.

Lil' Bobby was watching all of this from a treehouse in the yard. After a few minutes, his curiosity got the best of him, and he asked his father what he was doing.

"Well, son," replied Mr. Harold, "I look to see which way the nail is facing. If it's pointing towards the house, I use it. If not, I drop it in the bucket."

Lil' Bobby was confused, "But dad, what do you do with the other nails?"

Mr. Harold smiled and said, "Son, those are for the other side of the house."

32.

One day, Mr. Harold was sitting on a bench, chain-smoking through several cigarettes. A lady came up to him and asked what he was doing.

He replied, "Didn't you hear that smoking was good for your eyes?"

The lady frowned and said, that can't be. Cigarettes are bad all around.

Mr. Harold pointed to an ad in a magazine for cigarettes. "There you go," he said proudly, "It says right here, 'Try our cigarettes for thirty days and you'll *see*.'"

***

Mr. Harold was sitting with his neighbor who was complaining about married life. "Yes," the neighbor said, "I have a problem. My wife just started smoking."

"Well, maybe you should apply some lubrication?" Mr. Harold advised him.

***

Mr. Harold always believed cremation was the last chance for a smoking hot body.

33.

One day at work, Mr. Harold rode the elevator up to the twelfth floor and got out. The operator said, "Have a good day, son!"

Astonished, Mr. Harold said, "Um, I'm a little old to be your son."

Without missing a beat, the operator said, "I brought you up, didn't I?"

***

The next day Mr. Harold rode the elevator up to the eleventh floor and got out. He would have ridden to the twelfth floor but that's another story.

***

Mr. Harold loves to get on a crowded elevator and say, "I bet you're all wondering why I gathered you here today."

34.

Once upon a time, back in the old days of knights and castles, a Count named Mr. Harold the Sweettooth was arrested for stealing some tarts from the king's kitchen. The Count refused to tell the king where he had hidden all the delicacies, saying, "Mr. Harold be my name, and tart stealing be my game. Try as you will to be smart, you'll never find the royal tarts!"

The King was enraged and commanded, "Thy head shall be cut off from thy body if thou revealest not the location of my sweet tarts."

Still, the Count refused, saying, "Mr. Harold be my name, and tart stealing be my game. Try as you will to be smart, you'll never find the royal tarts!"

The king commanded to carry out the execution.

The poor Count lay his head on the chopping block. The Executioner raised his blade. The king then bellowed, "One...." And then "Two..." And finally, "Three..." The axe blade came down.

At the very last second, the Count cried out, "Stop! You've dodged my every evasion! I'll reveal the location!" But it was too late, the blade snipped off his head lickety-split.

The moral of the story: "Don't hatchet your counts before they chicken."

35.

Once upon a time, a royal knave named Mr. Harold the Fool stole a large golden throne from the king. He took the throne and displayed it prominently in the grass house he had built just outside the castle. He sat in it daily and pretended to be very important.

The king could not very well rule without a throne, so he had another one made. The knave promptly stole that one, placed it in his grass house next to the first, and had his wife sit in it as well.

The king was furious. His best men could not find the second throne, so he was forced to commission yet a third. And lo and behold, the knave stole it as well, and placed it in his grass house next to the first two.

The king called all his knights and all his foot soldiers and even mercenaries to find the thrones. Finally, one day, a soldier found the grass house and the incriminating evidence. They whisked the knave away and beheaded him in the town square.

The moral of the story: "People who live in grass houses should not stow thrones."

36.

One hot day in the Jungle in Africa, Mr. Harold, an explorer and mathematician, was assigned to follow a path through the wilds and to a village a few hours away. Because of the treacherous path and lack of modern conveniences like compasses, the natives would leave pints of whiskey along their paths to help measure the distances and not get lost. One could then take a snort or two of whiskey which would get him an hour down the path to the next bottle and so on, until a full pint was snorted. The pint, then, represented a very standard way of measurement for the natives. A village would be one pint or two pints, or even five pints away, and so forth.

Knowing this, Mr. Harold set out on his mission. Every now and again he would come across a flask, take a snort, and go on. However, about halfway a mean ole' hungry lion lay in his path. Poor Mr. Harold had no way to go around the lion. And to make matters worse, he had only enough whiskey to get him back to his starting point. Thus, he turned around.

Because he knew that the lion would still be in his way if he tried again, Mr. Harold did the only thing he could do. He called in a friend who had a World War 2 biplane. This friend strafed the poor lion from the sky. Thus, Mr. Harold made the journey, jumped over the dead lion's body, and completed his mission.

When he returned, he formulated his first mathematical postulate as follows:

"The snortest distance between two pints is a strafed lion."

37.

One day, Mr. Harold went to buy a new pair of shoes. The store clerk showed him several pairs, but none seemed to fit.

The clerk was exhausted and showed Mr. Harold his final pair. "They'll get looser once you walk in them a bit."

With a grimace, Mr. Harold told the clerk, "These shoes are so tight that I'll have to wear them four or five times before I can even try them on."

***

A few days later, one of Mr. Harold's friends asked how he was doing.

"Well," he replied, "I couldn't concentrate in the orange juice factory, I wasn't suited to be a good tailor, the muffler shop was exhausting, I couldn't cut it as a barber, I didn't have the patience to be a doctor, I didn't fit in at the shoe factory, pool maintenance was too draining, and I just don't see a future as a historian."

38.

Mr. Harold always fancied himself the most knowledgeable man in the church. One day, when the preacher was speaking about the evils of sports and betting, Mr. Harold stood up and said, "Preacher, I think you've got the Lord all wrong."

The preacher was red-faced and asked, "Whatever do you mean? God does not like sports and all the drunkenness and gambling associated with it."

Mr. Harold replied, "It says that God loved baseball right in the Bible."

The preacher, even angrier, replied, "Son, I've read the Bible from cover to cover and there is no mention of baseball."

"But you're wrong," said Mr. Harold, "It says so right here in Genesis that God created the Heavens and the Earth."

"What does that have to do with baseball???"

"He did it in the Big Inning…"

39.

At the end of a long sermon on a warm Sunday, the preacher was wrapping his sermon up by talking about Moses and how he was the perfect vessel to serve God. He then talked about his spat with Pharoah, how Moses led the Jews out of Egypt, and finally, how they wandered through the desert. All that time Moses continued to be the best example for the Jews to follow.

But Mr. Harold was twitching in his seat the entire time. He just couldn't hear another word and stood up, just as the preacher was at a critical moment in the story.

"I think you got it all wrong!" said Mr. Harold, interrupting the service. All eyes turned on him.

The preacher was red-faced but tried to remain calm. "Yes, my son?"

"Preacher, Moses was not a perfect man."

"Whatever do you mean?" exclaimed the exasperated Preacher.

Without missing a beat, Mr. Harold replied, "Well, he was the first man to break every one of God's commandments!"

"What???" exclaimed the preacher. Every mouth in the congregation was wide open.

"Yes," replied Mr. Harold, "He broke every one of God's commandments. In fact, he broke all ten Commandments at once!"

40.

Mr. Harold was sitting with his son, Lil' Bobby, one day. Mr. Harold began relating the following story.

"Two brothers, Pete and Re-Pete were in an airplane with parachutes on, waiting to skydive."

"Yes, papa," exclaimed Lil' Bobby intently listening to the story.

"And Pete jumped out. Who was left?"

Lil' Bobby proudly exclaimed, "Re-Pete!"

Mr. Harold started again, "OK, Pete and Re-Pete were in a plane and Pete jumped out. Who was left?"

Lil' Bobby, confused said again, "Re-Pete!"

"OK, Pete and Re-Pete were in a plane and Pete jumped out. Who was left???"

41.

Mr. Harold went to the podiatrist one day for a problem he was having with his feet. The Podiatrist examined his feet, thought awhile, and said, "Mr. Harold, I think I know what your problem is."

Mr. Harold was relieved. "What's wrong?"

The podiatrist stated, "Well, it's a minor infection."

He asked, "So, what's the treatment?"

The doctor told him, "It's actually quite easy. You simply need to put on a new pair of socks every day and you should have no more issues."

A few days passed and the phone rang in the podiatrist's office. The doctor answered. It was Mr. Harold.

"Doc, the infection has gotten a lot better. The only problem is, after putting on new socks every day, now I can't get my shoes on!"

42.

Once upon a time in the forest, a mama and a papa bear were worried that their son didn't like to eat meat. So, the papa bear showed the baby how to wade in the stream, roar a mighty roar, show his scary teeth, and then catch a salmon.

But alas, the baby bear showed no interest at all.

The mama bear then showed the baby bear how she could catch a deer. She stalked one from behind a bush, roared a mighty roar, showed her scary teeth, and then promptly caught the deer for supper.

The baby bear was excited now. He chased after a rabbit, showed it his scary teeth, and roared, "Give me your carrot!"

43.

Silly Suzie likes to recite the following poem:

Hickory, Dickory, Dock,

Two mice ran up the clock.

The clock struck one,

And the other got away.

***

When no one laughs, she recites the next one:

I dig, you dig, we dig.

He digs, you dig, they dig.

She knows it's not a beautiful poem, but it is deep.

***

Silly Sally asks Lil' Bobby, "You wanna hear a dirty joke?"

Lil' Bobby says, "Sure!"

"A boy slipped on a banana and fell in a mud hole!"

Lil' Bobby was angry and said, "That wasn't funny."

"Well," said Silly Sally, "Wanna hear a clean joke?"

"Sure."

"He then took a bath!"

44.

One day in school, Betty Joe was teaching class. The subject of the day was phonetic spelling. Betty called one of the pupils, Archibald Barisol, to the front. But Archibald was embarrassed and refused. Betty Joe let it slide and called Sam Jones up to the front to demonstrate.

Sam Jones stood in front of the class and said, "Sam Jones. Sam. Jones. S. A. M. You've got your Sam. J.O.N.E.S. You've got your Jones. You've got your Sam. You've got your Jones. You've got your Same Jones."

Better Joe was more than pleased and gave Sam a gold star.

"Archibald?" asked Betty Joe.

"No ma'am," he replied.

So, Betty Joe called Mary Smith to the front.

Mary stood in front of the class and said, "Mary Smith. Ma-Ree-Smith. M.A. You've got your 'Ma.' R.Y. You've got your 'ree.' You've got your Ma. You've got your Ree. Ma-Ree. S.M.I.T.H. you've got your Smith. You've got your Ma, you've got your Ree, you've got your Smith. You've got MARY SMITH."

"Very good!" exclaimed Betty Joe and gave her a star.

"Well, Archibald Barasol, it's your turn."

Archibald softly began. "A.R.C.H. You've got your Arch. I. You've got your I. B.A.L.D. You've got your 'bald.' You've got your Arch, you've got your I, you've got your Bald – ARCHIBALD. B.A.R. You've got your Bar. A.S. You've got your "Ass." O.L. You've got your "Ole". You've got your 'bare,' You've got your 'ass,' You've got your 'hole,' You've got your 'bald,' You've got your 'Bald Bear Ass Ole.' You've got your ARCHIBALD BARASOL."

Betty Joe, red-faced with embarrassment, gave him a star.

45.

It was a hot summer day. Mr. Harold was walking along the street and saw a nickel on the ground. He said, "It's so hot, I wouldn't even bend over for a nickel."

Then Mr. Harold thought a bit, reached into his pocket, and pulled out a dime. He then promptly threw it down by the nickel.

"Now," he said, "I would bend over for 15 cents."

***

Mr. Harold rapid fired the following questions to his son:

"Boy, where does a vampire keep his money?"

"In a blood bank, dad," the boy replied.

"Where does a penguin keep his money?"

"In a snow-bank!"

"Where do fish keep their money?"

"In a river-bank."

"And where can one always find money"

"In the dictionary!"

46.

Betty Joe came home one day very distraught. Mr. Harold asked her what was wrong.

"Well," she started, "I've just had the worst news ever."

"Oh, no. What's that, dear?"

Betty Joe explained, "I went to the dentist for a check-up."

Mr. Harold looked puzzled, "And what's wrong with that?"

Betty Joe was on the point of tears, "And he found a lump in my breast."

***

Betty Joe told her husband. "I really like that dentist. He's won so many awards."

"How do you know that?" Mr. Harold asked.

"Cuz' on his wall is a little plague."

47.

Mr. Harold was sitting with his son, Lil' Bobby, fishing at the edge of the lake. "Son," he asked, "Did you hear about the poor cow who had an abortion?"

"No, dad," replied his son.

"The cow was decaffeinated."

Lil' Bobby replied, "To be udderly honest, I'm afraid you butchered that one!"

Mr. Harold tried again, "Son, what did the mama cow say to the baby cow?"

Lil' Bobby was stumped.

"It's pasture bedtime."

48.

Betty Joe was walking along a little stream, trying to find a way to cross it without getting wet. On the other side of the stream was a lady also walking. Betty Joe yelled out, "Ma'am, how do I get to the other side of the creek?"

The lady replied, "You're already *on* the other side of the creek."

***

Mr. Harold teased his wife when she got home. He asked, "What do you get when you cross a river and a stream?"

Betty Joe could not answer.

"Wet," he said.

***

He then asked his wife why she had brought pen and paper to the creek,

She said, "Well, cuz' I saw a sign that said 'Draw Bridge!'"

49.

Mr. Harold the Astronaut was in his space capsule that just landed on the surface of Mars. He did the final checks and exited the capsule. After looking around a bit, he contacted Houston to let them know he'd arrive.

However, Mr. Harold looked up and this exquisite, fifteen-foot-tall, green space lady walked up to him with a smile. The lady said, "You'd probably like me to take you to our leader?"

Mr. Harold shook his head as he looked up at the giant lady. He said coyly, "Take me to your ladder, I'll see your leader later."

***

Mr. Harold asked the alien, "Why didn't you come visit the earth?"

The alien replied, "Well, when I looked it up it only had one star."

***

"But you really should visit us sometime," Mr. Harold pleaded.

The alien thought a bit and said, "OK, I'll planet."

50.

Lil' Bobby was riding in a small red wagon that was pulled by a scraggly kid goat. Lil' Bobby had just been to the dentist and was having trouble speaking. He came up to a young girl in pigtails. Lil' Bobby greeted her, saying, "Woe Dote! Dit' in Dirl!" The girl promptly got in the wagon. Then Lil' Bobby called out, "Ditty up, Dote." And off they went.

A bit down the road Lil' Bobby asked the girl for a kiss. The girl slapped him for his impudence. He said, "Woe Dote! Dit out Dirl!" At which point the girl jumped out of the wagon in a huff. Lil' Bobby then commanded the goat, "Ditty up, Dote." And so, the goat pulled the wagon further.

Up ahead Lil' Bobby saw another cute little girl. Once he had pulled next to her, he said, "Woe Dote! Dit in Dirl!" The girl got in the wagon. Yet again, Lil' Bobby asked her for a kiss at which point she slapped him on his other cheek. He called out, "Woe Dote! Dit out Dirl!" The girl got out of the wagon and scurried home not looking behind her. Lil' Bobby barked again, "Ditty up, Dote," and off they went.

Lil' Bobby came upon a third girl. He said, "Woe, Dote! Dit in Dirl!" She jumped in just as he exclaimed, "Ditty up, Dote." Lil' Bobby asked the third girl for a Kiss whereupon she also slapped him.

Lil' Bobby angrily said, "Woe Dote! Dit out, Dirl!" The third girl left offended. Lil' Bobby called out, "Ditty up, Dote," and off he went.

Lil' Bobby went a little farther, thought awhile, and said, "Woe Dote! Dit in Dote. Diddy up, Dote!"

51.

Once, when Lil' Bobby was in third grade, he was taking a final test just before the Christmas break. The test was full of math, English, history, and social studies questions. Because he hadn't studied, Lil' Bobby wrote in big letters across the exam God knows the answers to all these questions! Merry Christmas!

After the Christmas break, the teacher handed Lil' Bobby his graded test. In bright red letters across the top was, "God made an "A." You got an "F." Happy New year!

***

Lil' Bobby asked his teacher, "Knock, knock."

"Who's there?" she asked.

"A broken pencil."

"A broken pencil who?"

"Never mind. It's pointless!"

52.

Lil' Bobby was in his freshman year of college when he wrote home to his dad, Mr. Harold. The letter said, "No Mon, no Fun, your Son."

Mr. Harold wrote back, "Too Bad, how Sad, your Dad."

***

The boy came home for Christmas vacation, but nothing seemed to satisfy him. "Dad," said Lil' Bobby, "I'm cold."

Mr. Harold replied, "Go stand in the corner, then."

"But why, dad?"

"Because it's 90° there!"

53.

Mr. Harold loved to practice all his jokes in the chicken coop. He had them laying in the aisles.

He always started with, "Why did the chicken cross the road?"

When the chickens didn't say anything, he would answer, "Because it was too far to go around."

*****

Then he would ask, "What do you call a bird that's afraid to fly?"

"A chicken!" they clucked.

*****

The chickens got their revenge and asked, "Why did the young rooster tell such bad jokes?

Mr. Harold was stumped.

"Like feather, like son," they answered.

54.

Once upon a time, there were three monkeys that lived in a thirteen-story hotel. They each had a room on the 13th floor. The first monkey rode the elevator to his room, climbed out of the window, and slid down a flagpole all the way to the bottom. As he slid, he hollered, "Wwweeeee" all the way down."

The second monkey saw how much fun this was, so he rode up the elevator to the 13th floor, went into his room, and climbed out the window. He cracked his knuckles and slid down this flagpole just like the first monkey. He hollered "Woopeeeeeeeeeeee!" all the way down.

The third monkey saw this and just couldn't resist. He rode up the elevator to the 13th floor, went into his room, and climbed out the window. He cracked his knuckles and slid down the flagpole. As he went down, he yelled, "Radiooooooo!"

55.

Betty Joe was leading her little weenie dog down the sidewalk one fine day. As she passed a bum on the street, the little dog raised up its hind leg near the man. The man jumped back in fear.

Betty Joe said, "Don't worry, sir. He won't bite."

The bum replied, "Oh, I thought he was going to kick me!"

***

Betty Joe was talking with her preacher, praising her weenie dog. "My dog is so smart!"

"Really? How so?" the preacher asked.

"I asked him what's two plus two? He said nothing."

56.

Mr. Harold was lying drunk on the sidewalk in front of his own home. He moaned and struggled but could not get up. A kindly police officer came up to him and asked him what he was doing there.

Mr. Harold slurred, "If I can get over this fence, I'm going inside my house."

The police officer said, "Buddy, I think you need a breathalyzer."

Mr. Harold asked, "What's that?"

"Well," replied the officer, "it's a bag that tells when you've drunk too much."

"Well, whadya' know," countered Mr. Harold, "I've been married to one of those for years!"

57.

Having been plagued by burglars, Mr. Harold bought himself a young watchdog that he named Fido. Every day, Mr. Harold trained Fido to attack at his command using a small ball. He would yell, "Attack!" and the little dog would tear the ball to pieces. Soon, the little dog had become a ferocious guardian.

One balmy night a burglar broke into Mr. Harold's house. But Mr. Harold was ready for just such an occasion as was Fido. As soon as the burglar stepped through his window, Mr. Harold yelled, "ATTACK!" The little dog jumped up, growled like a monster, and tore the training ball to pieces.

58.

Mr. Harold was driving his car one day alongside an insane asylum when he had a flat tire. Mr. Harold rolled up his sleeves and got to work on the repair. As he removed the tire, he unfortunately misplaced the lug nuts. He looked everywhere for the darned things. He simply didn't know what had become of them.

An inmate at the asylum had been watching Mr. Harold changing the tire the whole time. The inmate had a suggestion. Why couldn't Mr. Harold just take one lug nut off each of the other wheels to use?

Mr. Harold shrugged his shoulders and set about collecting one lug nut from each of the other tires. In no time flat, he had repaired the wheel. Mr. Harold then asked the inmate, why, if he was so smart, was he in an insane asylum.

The inmate replied, "I may be crazy but I'm not stupid."

59.

One fall day, a piece of string walked into a tavern and ordered a drink. The tavern owner said, "We don't serve strings in here," and tossed him out.

The string was angry. He went tied himself up in a knot and walked straight back into the tavern and ordered a drink. The tavern owner again said, "I done told you before, we don't serve strings in here," and tossed him out a second time.

Not to be deterred, the string frayed up his hair, went back into the tavern, and again ordered a drink. The tavern owner shook his head and angrily asked, "Aren't you the same string that I just tossed out twice?"

The string confidently responded, "Nope, I'm a frayed knot."

60.

After an accident, Mr. Harold went to see his family doctor. The doctor asked, "What seems to be the trouble?"

Mr. Harold replied, "My arm's broken in two places."

The doctor looked him over and said, "If you want my advice, I'd stay out of those two places."

***

Mr. Harold woke up in a hospital after a serious accident. "Hey, doctor! I can't feel my legs!"

The doctor smiled and said, "I know, I amputated your arms!"

***

Mr. Harold was talking to the doctor. "I'll never forget my dad's last words."

The doctor said, "What were they?"

Mr. Harold replied, "Oh, no! It's a bus!"

61.

A few days later, Mr. Harold had a stroke and went back to the family doctor. The doctor asked, "Mr. Harold, what seems to be the problem this time?"

Mr. Harold said, "When I lift my right arm like this over my head it hurts."

The doctor thought a minute and said, "If I were you, I'd stop lifting my right arm over my head."

***

Lil' Bobby was walking with his father and asked, "Dad, if I told you I was gay, would you still love me?"

"Don't be silly, son," Mr. Harold replied. "You were an accident. I never loved you in the first place."

62.

Once upon a time a preacher owned a stubborn donkey that he used on his missions to carry equipment and to ride. Even though the donkey was stubborn, it had been trained to go when the minister would say, "Praise the Lord!" and it would stop when he would say, "Amen." No matter what else you would say to the old donkey, it only responded to those two commands.

One day Mr. Harold was going camping in the mountains and wanted to borrow the preacher's donkey. The preacher explained how to make the donkey go or stop. This seemed easy to Mr. Harold, so he set off on his trip.

With Mr. Harold riding on top, they set off on a narrow trail. Just to be sure, Mr. Harold told the donkey, "Amen," and the donkey stopped. Then he said, "Praise the Lord," and the donkey started walking again. This really tickled Mr. Harold, so much so, that he said "Praise the Lord" again. The donkey started trotting. Unfortunately, just up ahead was a sheer cliff.

Mr. Harold was in a panic and tugged on the reins, hollering "Woah! Woah!" but the donkey didn't even slow down. Just in time, Mr. Harold remembered the command word and said, "Amen." The Donkey came to an abrupt halt. One more step and the two would have gone right over the cliff. Mr. Harold looked up to Heaven, wiped his brow, and said, "Praise the Lord!"

63.

Sometimes Mr. Harold will recite the following poem:

A Man,

A Miss,

A Car,

A Curve,

He kissed the Miss,

and Missed the Curve.

***

Betty Joe in a huff told Mr. Harold, "I felt incomplete until I married you. Now I'm finished!"

***

A few minutes later, Mr. Harold responds, "Every man wants a beautiful wife, a smart wife, a loving wife, a sexy wife, and a cooperative wife. Sadly, bigamy is illegal!"

64.

Unfortunately, Mr. Harold came down with a very serious illness and needed medical treatment. He went to the family doctor. While he was lying on the examining bed, the doctor told Betty Joe, his wife, "Alas, I can give him some medicine but that will only give him six months to live."

Betty Joe was in tears. "I don't know what to do, Doc. We don't have the money to pay you."

The doctor responded, "Then, I'll give him a year left to live."

***

Mr. Harold sat with the doctor. "Doc, I've got a problem. I gave my wife a glue stick instead of chapstick."

"And what's wrong with that?" he asked.

"She's still not talking to me."

65.

Being a keen mathematician, Mr. Harold likes to tell where the real Pythagorean theorem originated.

Long ago, on the American plains, the Indians had the custom to choose the sex of their baby. When the squaw was ready to deliver, she sent out her brave into the wild. If he killed a bear, he would skin in, lay out the fur, place the squaw on it, and the next morning she would have a little boy. If he killed a deer, he would skin that, lay out the fur, place the squaw on it, and she would have a little girl.

One day, a squaw was ready to deliver, so she sent out her brave in the wild. However, this brave had no luck. He found neither bear, nor deer, nor anything else around. However, the brave did stumble upon a traveling circus going across the west that happened to have a hippopotamus. So, he did the next best thing, killed the hippo, skinned, it, placed his squaw on the pelt, and waited. The next day to his surprise she had twins.

Thereafter, it was repeated from Chief to tribe for ages: The sons of the squaws on the hippopotamus are equal to the sons of the squaws on the other two hides.

66.

It was a bad day for Mr. Harold when he was arrested and sentenced to five years for a minor crime. As he sat at the mess table with the other prisoners, he noticed that it was very quiet. Suddenly, one of the prisoners stood up and yelled, "37!" All the prisoners laughed except for Mr. Harold, who had no idea what was going on.

A few minutes later someone stood up and yelled, "22!" and all the prisoners laughed.

Mr. Harold was most perplexed. He poked his neighbor and asked what the numbers meant. The old prisoner said, "Well, we be in here so long, that we know each other's jokes. Now, all we must do is say the number, we remember the joke, and we laugh."

Mr. Harold thought this was pretty clever. He decided to give it a try. He stood up and called out "75!" But no one laughed. He looked around and said, "48!" Again, no one laughed. Mr. Harold sat down in disappointment.

He turned to the old prisoner and asked, "What just happened? I thought all the jokes had numbers."

The old prisoner shook his head and said, "Some folks just can't tell a joke."

67.

Mr. Harold had been in prison for several months and wanted to escape. He and his cellmate made elaborate plans, dug night and day with a spoon, and eventually, made it out to the prison wall which was several dozen yards above the ground. They didn't know what to do.

The cellmate told Mr. Harold, "Look, I'll shine this flashlight down to the ground below, and you slide down the beam."

Mr. Harold shook his head, "Not on your life! I'd get halfway down and you'd turn off the light!"

***

Mr. Harold spent several more years trying to tunnel out of the prison. At last, he made it and yelled, "I'm free! I'm free!"

Lil' Bobby was standing nearby and replied, "That's not a big deal. I'm four!"

68.

Mr. Harold was just starting his first job as a truck driver. He was having an awfully hard time starting his truck. He ground the gears, causing a hideous scraping sound.

Another driver who was working on his own truck called over to him, "You have to double clutch it!"

Mr. Harold replied, "You can't fool me! One of those pedals is the brake."

69.

Lil' Bobby was sitting with his father, Mr. Harold, on the porch. With an evil grin, he asked, "Pops, what is green, when it grows gets about six inches tall, and has red wheels?"

Mr. Harold was perplexed. "No idea, son."

Lil' Bobby replied, "It's 'Grass.' I just put the red wheels to fool you."

***

Seeing the boy was perplexed, Mr. Harold said, "The other day I was in the bar when a grasshopper came in."

"Oh, really? What happened?" asked the boy.

"Well," replied Mr. Harold, "While I was sitting at the bar, the bartender told him, 'Hey, we've got a drink named after you.'"

"What happened next"

"The grasshopper replied, 'Wow! That's crazy that you have a drink named Stanley!'"

70.

One afternoon, Mr. Harold was walking down the sidewalk with a yellow banana in his ear. A small boy came up to him and tugged on his trousers, curious about the banana in his ear. "Mista! Mista! Whatcha' doin'?"

Mr. Harold ignored him. But the small boy kept tugging on his trousers and asking. "Mista! Mista! Whatcha' doin' with that banana in your ear?"

Mr. Harold walked on.

The little boy gave another tug, "Mista! Mista! Whatcha' doin' wit' dat banana in your ear?"

Mr. Harold looked down and said, "Sorry, son. I can't hear a word you are saying cuz' of this banana I have in my ear."

71.

Mr. Harold loves to leave a room thinking with gems such as these:

Do you realize that the higher a man climbs up the ladder, the more of his rear he shows?

A person who stands on a toilet is high on pot.

A man who walks in front of a car gets tired, but when he walks behind it, he gets exhausted.

A guy who sneezes without a tissue takes matters into his own hands.

The man who laughs last didn't get the joke.

War doesn't determine who is right, but who is left.

A fly that rests on a toilet seat is liable to get pissed off.

72.

One day Lil' Bobby was on his way to school and had to climb through a fence. In the process, he caught his pants and tore a hole clean through. He tried to fix the hole with a safety pin, but that made him late for school. When he finally arrived, the teacher said, "Lil' Bobby, I see you're a little behind."

Lil' Bobby blushed as he replied, "Sorry, Teach! I thought I had that pinned up."

***

Lil' Bobby's teacher told him, "Young man, do you know what the word 'tardy' means?"

"No, teacher. You must've covered that before I got here."

***

The next day the teacher asked, "Do you have a good excuse for being absent yesterday?"

Lil' Bobby answered, "If I had a good excuse, I'd save it and use it tomorrow!"

73.

Mr. Harold was on a tractor riding with his son, Lil' Bobby. "Son," he asked, "How do farmers break up with their girlfriends?"

Lil' Bobby scratched his head and answered, "I dunno, pops."

Mr. Harold replied, "With John Deere letters!"

***

Mr. Harold then asked his son, "Boy, what are farmers attracted to the most?

Lil' Bobby was stumped again.

Mr. Harold answered, "A nice dairy air."

74.

One evening, Mr. Harold was in bed with his wife, Betty Joe, smoking a cigarette. He had such a bad habit that there was almost no time he didn't have one in his mouth puffing away.

Betty Joe put her magazine down and looked over at him. "One day," she started, "You smoke so much you're gonna' die with a cigarette in your mouth!" Mr. Harold ignored her and puffed away happily.

Later that evening, while the couple was still watching TV in bed, a burglar broke in and demanded money. Mr. Harold refused, so the burglar shot him, the cigarette still in the corner of his mouth.

Betty Joe looked over at him in disgust, "I told ya' so!"

75.

Mr. Harold wants to know,

   If a King sits on "Gold," who sits on "Silver?"

***

Once upon a time two of the king's servants found the king's dead body in bed with a large sword sticking out of his chest. One servant turned to the other and said, "Boy, he must have had a bad knight!"

76.

Once upon a time, there was a very backward and illiterate lad named Bobby who fell in love with a beautiful neighbor girl, Tammy Sue. The two went out for a while and Bobby was over the moon about the girl. However, one day, he opened his mailbox and saw a "Dear John" letter. The girl wanted nothing more to do with Bobby and refused to see him, saying everything was explained in the letter. However, the boy couldn't read a word.

Not knowing what he had done wrong to lose Tammy Sue, he showed the letter to his mother so she could read it to him. She opened the letter and started reading aloud, "Dear Bobby..." But then Bobby's mother stopped as she read ahead. Her eyes grew big, her lips tensed, and her cheeks flushed. Before reading another word, she thrust the letter back in Bobby's hands and said, "Get outa' my house, boy! I don't ever want to see you again!"

Bobby was in shock. What could the letter have said? He gathered his meager belongings and headed out the door. As he was leaving, he saw his father pull up in a pickup truck. He explained what had happened and asked his dad to read the letter to him. His father opened the letter and started to read, "Dear Bobby..." But as before, he paused, read ahead a bit, and became visibly furious. He, too, thrust the letter back at Bobby and commanded him off his farm. He was no longer his son.

More frustrated than ever, Bobby left. He knew a friend up the road who would never think anything bad about him, so he decided to show the letter to him. Perhaps then he would know the contents of Tammy Sue's letter. And so, explaining the situation, his friend agreed. Again, as before, "Dear Bobby." But the friend also stopped, read ahead, became angered, and commanded Bobby out of his sight forever more.

This went on a few more times until Bobby got the idea that he shouldn't show the letter to anyone. He just couldn't risk it. He'd lost his parents, his best friend, his preacher, his barber, and even his Sunday School teacher all in the same manner. Without any options, he decided to join the Navy, forget his troubles, and see the world. But he always kept the letter with him, in hopes that one day he would be able to read it for himself. And he never forgot about Tammy Sue.

It just so happened one night when he was on the deck of a large ship on a mission to the Persian Gulf that he heard about another sailor on board who had something of the opposite problem as Bobby. The sailor could read, but he couldn't understand a word he was reading. This was perfect! Bobby asked the sailor that very night to read him the letter out loud.

The two met outside in an isolated part of the ship overlooking the vast ocean and the lovely moon that was rising. The sailor took the letter, put on his reading glasses, and started very slowly to read out loud. "D-d-d-d-dear Bobobobobbby...." The anticipation could not have been higher.

But just as he started, a huge gust of wind kicked up and tore the letter from the sailor's hand. It floated away in the wind never to be seen again.

78.

Mr. Harold got a job driving a bus. It was his first day of work and he didn't know exactly what to expect. When he saw the bus, it was big and yellow, just like Big Bird. He shrugged his shoulders and took off.

At his first stop, two very corpulent women got on. Mr. Harold asked their names. They both said, "Patty." Mr. Harold shrugged and gestured them to the back of the bus. They waddled their way back, giggling the whole time.

At the next stop, a very simple boy got on. Mr. Harold asked his name. The boy replied, "Russ," but my parents call me "Special Russ" cuz' I'm special." Mr. Harold shrugged and drove on.

At the third stop, a skinny hipster got on. Mr. Harold asked his name. The man replied, "Breeze, man…Leonard Breeze." Mr. Harold shrugged, asked him to take a seat, and drove on.

A few streets later and Mr. Harold heard a commotion behind him. When he looked in his mirror, both ladies named Patty were pointing at Leonard Breeze who was playing with his bare feet. "It's so gross!" they squealed. Mr. Harold asked Leonard to stop picking at his feet. He then shrugged and drove on.

Finally, he came to the last stop. All the passengers got off. Mr. Harold was tired and went straight home. When he got in the door, his wife asked him how his day was.

Mr. Harold said, "I had two obese Patties, Special Russ, Leonard Breeze pickin' bunions on a Sesame Street bus."

79.

Lil' Bobby loves soda. Whenever he asks his dad, Mr. Harold, for a drink, he always hears the following:

One day, when the Mountain Dew was fresh on the lawn, and the tops of the trees were Sunkist, Pepsi Cola asked Mr. Pibb where he could meet someone nice. Mr. Pibb introduced him to Coca-Cola. They hit it off and right away decided they wanted to have a little Squirt. Not knowing much about the birds and the bees, they went to Dr. Pepper.

Dr. Pepper took one look at them and laughed, saying, "You guys can't have a little Squirt! You're both pops."

81.

One day while Mr. Harold was shaving, he sneezed violently. It was so sudden and powerful that his razor cut off his nose and his toe. Mr. Harold stood in shock, not knowing what to do. Fortunately, there was some Super Glue in the medicine cabinet, so he reattached them both.

Unfortunately, Mr. Harold got mixed up and glued his toe where his nose should be and his nose where his toe should be. Everything seemed fine except now his nose runs and his toe smells. Oh, and when he sneezes he blows off his sock.

***

Mr. Harold told his son, "Someone I know spends all day shaving and still has a beard."

"Really dad? How's that possible?"

"He's the barber."

82.

Mr. Harold asked his son, Lil' Bobby, "Son, who is bigger, Mr. Bigger or Mr. Bigger's baby?"

Lil' Bobby thought and thought but could only say, "Gee, dad, I don't know."

Mr. Harold smiled and said, "Of course, it's the baby. He's a *little* Bigger.

***

Lil' Bobby thought he was being clever and asked his dad, "When does a joke become a dad joke?"

Mr. Harold replied, "When it becomes apparent."

***

The teacher called Lil' Bobby's house and asked, "You say your son has a cold and can't come to school today? To whom am I speaking?"

"This is my father."

83.

Mr. Harold went into a bar one day with his dog Fido. He told the barkeep that he didn't have any money, but he had a dog that could talk. He bet the barkeep that if Fido could answer questions, he would get a free drink. The barkeep reluctantly agreed.

Mr. Harold asked, "What's on top of this building that keeps the inside dry from rain?"

Fido barked, "Roof!"

Mr. Harold said, "See there? He said roof."

The barkeep was not amused. "Before I give you a free drink, he'd better talk!"

Mr. Harold asked the dog a second question, "Fido, who's the best baseball player who ever lived?"

Fido barked, "Roof! Roof!"

Mr. Harold said, "See there? He said 'Babe Ruth!'"

The barkeep promptly tossed Mr. Harold and Fido on the street.

Mr. Harold sat on the ground with his head in his hands. The dog looked over and said, "I guess I should've said Mickey Mantle."

84.

One day Mr. Harold was training to swim the English Channel, a grueling 20.5 mile swim separating England and France. He trained night and day, day and night. On the morning of his swim, his whole family came out to cheer him on. Mr. Harold was tickled pink as he dove into the frigid water and started swimming toward France.

Unfortunately, Mr. Harold was not the best swimmer. He got about fifteen miles into the swim when he started getting tired. So, he turned around and swam back.

***

A few years later a reporter was interviewing Mr. Harold about his swimming career and asked him what his favorite stroke was.

Without missing a beat, he replied, "The one that did in my mother-in-law."

85.

Mr. Harold asked his witless son, Lil' Bobby, "Son, how do you catch a *'unique'* rabbit?"

Lil' Bobby didn't have an answer.

Mr. Harold replied, "You 'nique' up on him." He continued, "And how do you catch a 'tame' rabbit?

Lil' Bobby was dumbfounded.

Mr. Harold replied, "The *'tame'* way."

***

Lil' Bobby asked his mom, Betty Joe, "How do you catch a rabbit?"

Betty Joe replied, "Well, I guess you have to throw it first."

86.

One hot summer day Mr. Harold was working in the field with an old dirty farmer. The sun was brutally beating down and it was as hot as an oven. Mr. Harold decided he needed a drink of water. He looked around and the only cup he saw was the farmer's coffee cup. Just like the farmer, the cup was dirty, filthy, and covered in tobacco juice. In short, it was repulsive. However, there was one small clean spot on the rim in an inconvenient location.

Mr. Harold was so thirsty, that he decided to pick up the cup by the handle and fill it with water. But he was not going to drink from the dirty portion. He twisted and bent his arm like a pretzel until at last, he could drink from that one clean spot.

The farmer looked at the ridiculous sight and said, "Hey, that's funny. That's exactly how I drink from that cup!"

87.

Mr. Harold was sitting on his porch one day with an old friend of his, George. Mr. Harold began to complain, "Boy, kids are dumb!"

George agreed, "They sure are dumb, Mr. Harold. Why, the other day my son comes home from college spouting his book-learnin!'"

Mr. Harold asked, "Like what?"

George says, "He tells me in math class they learned 'pi R squared.'"

Mr. Harold replies, "That's stupid. Everyone knows pie are round."

***

A little later, Mr. Harold told George, "You know what that silly boy of mine wants to do?"

George replied, "No tellin.'"

Mr. Harold replied, "He wants to go to clown college!"

George snickered, "People would only laugh at 'im!"

88.

It was a hot day in the middle of the Sahara as Mr. Harold, and two of his friends, George and Tim were walking, about to die from the heat. When they were about to expire, Tim finds a magic lamp.

They all three rub the lamp at once and a beautiful genie appears before them. "I thank you for releasing me from my bondage," the genie said. "As a token of my gratitude I shall grant you each one wish."

Tim decided to go first. "I wish to have a tall jug of water so I can make it across this desert."

The genie replied, "Your wish is my command!" And so it was, a tall jug of cool, refreshing water stood in front of Tim.

George decided to go next. "I wish to have a large bountiful feast in order that I might make it across the desert."

The genie replied, "Your wish is my command!" And so it was, a large table of exotic and delicious foods and wine lay spread before George.

Mr. Harold decided to go last. "I wish to have a car door!"

The genie raised an eyebrow and asked, "A car door? What on earth for?"

Mr. Harold replied with a gleam in his eye, "In case it gets hot I can roll down the window!"

89.

Mr. Harold and two of his friends, Tim and George, were aboard a ship when it hit something and started to sink. The three made it into a life raft along with the captain of the boat. However, the life raft was only designed for three people and was taking on water rapidly.

The captain had a suggestion. He would ask each of them a question. If they answered correctly, they could stay on. If they answered incorrectly, the person would have to jump out and take his own chances. The three agreed.

The captain asked Tim, "What was the worst sea disaster in history?"

Tim thought and thought and finally replied, "The Titanic!"

The captain agreed. He then asked George, "About how many people died on the fateful day when the Titanic went down?"

George thought and thought and finally replied, "About 1500?"

The captain said, "Close enough. You can stay." He then turned to Mr. Harold and said, "Name them!"

90.

One day Mr. Harold went to the family doctor because he wasn't losing weight on his new diet. The doctor looked him over and advised, "I recommend running 5 miles every day. That should do the trick."

Mr. Harold smiled and left the office, determined to follow the doctor's advice.

A week later Mr. Harold called the doctor on the phone with a complaint.

The doctor asked, "What's wrong? Didn't you follow my advice to run 5 miles every day?"

Mr. Harold said, "Yes, I did that. And I lost some weight!"

The doctor was perplexed, "Well, what seems to be the problem?"

Mr. Harold replied, "Now I'm thirty-five miles from home!"

91.

Mr. Harold was walking down the street one day when he came upon a boy selling "Smart Pills" on the street. He asked the boy, "Are these guaranteed to make you smarter?"

The boy happily replied, "Yes, they are…or your money back."

Mr. Harold thought, "Well, they're only a nickel. What's there to lose?"

So, he bought five and promptly put them in his mouth. Immediately he spat them out of his mouth. "Yuck! Those aren't smart pills! Those are rabbit poops!"

The little boy smiled, "See? You're getting smarter already."

92.

Mr. Harold was out fishing with his friend George who happened to be a game warden. They were on a small boat in the middle of the lake when Mr. Harold dug into his bag and pulled out a stick of dynamite. Before George could stop him, Mr. Harold lit the dynamite and tossed it into the lake. It exploded and several fish floated up to the top of the water.

George screamed, "That's illegal! You can't do that!"

Mr. Harold lit another stick of dynamite and handed it to George. He coyly asked, "You here to fish or to talk?"

93.

Mr. Harold likes to play poker. When he's at the table he makes everyone laugh with the following:

A gambler bet his girlfriend she wouldn't marry him.

She called his bet and raised him five.

***

Mr. Harold came home and his wife, Betty Joe was angry. "Where have you been!?!" she asked angrily.

Mr. Harold replied, "Sorry, honey, I lost you in a poker game. You're gonna' have to leave."

Betty Joe was furious, "How did you manage that, you fool?"

Mr. Harold replied, "It wasn't easy. I had to fold a royal flush."

94.

Mr. Harold and his friend George were sitting on the porch, watching the neighborhood. Mr. Harold turned to George and said, "Boy, I'll tell ya'! I just got this new hearing aid. I haven't heard this good in twenty years!"

George asked, "That's great! What kind is it?"

Mr. Harold replied, "10:30."

***

A few minutes later George asked, "Do you wear boxers or briefs?"

Mr. Harold replied, "Depends…"

95.

Mr. Harold was at the circus one day when he noticed a large carnie standing in front of three colorful circus tents. The carnie told Mr. Harold that within each tent was a challenge. Whoever could complete all three challenges would get free tickets to the circus for life.

Mr. Harold was intrigued. "What are the challenges, my good man?"

The carnie smiled and said, "Inside the first tent is a casket of the finest whiskey money can buy. You must drink it all down!"

Mr. Harold smiled as he knew this would be easy.

The carnie continued, "Inside the second tent is the most vicious lion man has ever seen. But the poor beast has a thorn in its paw and is in terrible pain. You must remove this thorn be mindful that the lion will gobble you up as soon as look at you!"

The carnie continued, "Inside the third tent is a ferocious Amazonian lady, never tamed by man. You must bed her."

Mr. Harold lifted an eyebrow, but he was up for the challenge. He entered the first tent and was there for quite some time. Just as the carnie started to worry, out staggered Mr. Harold, as drunk as he had ever been. He was so plastered, that the carnie had to point him towards the second tent or he wouldn't have made it.

Several minutes passed. The shocked carnie sat by the tent opening aghast as the most ferocious roars and growls came from the tent. He was sure Mr. Harold was a goner.

But then, it was quiet. Mr. Harold emerged, scratched and bloody. Still drunk, he stammered, "Now where's the lady with the thorn in her foot?"

96.

Mr. Harold was in a bar one day but didn't have any money for a drink. He whispered to the bartender, "Hey, buddy! See that horse over there? If I can make him laugh, will you give me a free drink?"

The bartender agreed.

Mr. Harold went over to the horse and whispered in the horse's ear. The bartender was more than curious but was too far away to hear anything. Pretty soon, the horse started laughing and laughing. Mr. Harold came back and demanded his drink.

"Now wait just a minute!" exclaimed the bartender, "Something's not right. You're pulling a fast one on me."

Mr. Harold smiled, "OK, double or nothing. I bet I can now make him cry and you give me two beers!"

"Deal!" exclaimed the curious bartender.

So, Mr. Harold walked over to the horse and whispered in his ear some more. Lo and behold, the horse started to weep like a baby.

After pouring the two drinks, the bartender could take no more and asked, "So what did you say to that horse to make him laugh?"

Mr. Harold said, "I whispered to it that I had a bigger thing than he did."

The bartender followed up, "And what made him cry?"

Mr. Harold smiled, "When I showed him it was true!"

97.

One day Mr. Harold was in London and was watching two royal guards standing at attention. However, one was getting chewed out by his superior.

The commander said, "So, soldier! You know as well as I do, we are ordered not to move, not so much as twitch while we are on duty!"

"Yes, sir," stated the guard meekly.

"So why I did see you twitch!?!"

"Well, sir, you see, a small squirrel came right up to me and ran up me right pant leg!"

"So, is that why you twitched!?!"

"No sir, tis' not."

"Then why did you twitch!?!"

"Well, sir, you see, another small squirrel came up to me and ran up me left pant leg!"

"So, is *that* why you twitched?

"Well, no sir."

"So bloody 'ell, why on earth did you twitch!?!"

"Well, sir, it's when I 'eard one of 'em say to the other, 'Let's eat one now and save one 'til later.'"

98.

One day, Mr. Harold and his son were out on the farm. He asked Lil' Bobby, "So, son, how can you tell if a little chick is a boy or a girl?"

Lil' Bobby was stumped as usual, "I dunno', dad."

Mr. Harold cuddled the little chick in his palm and blew on the fluffy bird. "That's how," he said with a smile.

***

With a twinkle in his eye, Mr. Harold then asked his son, "What do you call a bird that is afraid to fly?"

Lil' Bobby was stumped.

Mr. Harold answered, "Chicken!"

99.

One day, Mr. Harold was at the barber. His son, Lil' Bobby, was walking by and saw his dad sitting in the chair. He ran up to his dad and asked, "Papa, are you getting a haircut?"

Mr. Harold smiled and said, "No, I'm getting them *all* cut!"

***

Mr. Harold wanted his son to get his hair cut, but the boy refused, asking, "What if I don't like the cut?"

Mr. Harold replied, "Don't worry, son. It'll grow on you!"

Made in the USA
Coppell, TX
28 April 2023

16182163R00128